PERCY's London

St. Paul's Cathedral

The Tower of London

Victoria Embankment

Euston Rd.

Charing Cross Rd.

Piccadilly Circus

Trafalgar Sq.

The Mall

Big Ben

Houses of Parliament

Westminster Abbey

Albert Embankment

Vauxhall Bridge

Tower Bridge Rd.

Tower Bridge

PERCY *to the* RESCUE

Steven J. Simmons • Illustrated by Kim Howard

TALEWINDS
A Charlesbridge Imprint

A *TALEWINDS* Book
Published by Charlesbridge Publishing
85 Main Street, Watertown, MA 02172-4411
(617) 926-0329

Library of Congress Cataloging-in-Publication Data
Simmons, Steven J., 1946-
Percy to the rescue / Steven J. Simmons; illustrated by Kim Howard.
p. cm.
"A Talewinds Book."
Summary: A pigeon who loves flying around London
enjoying the sights finds a way to help two boys who
are stranded on an island in Hyde Park.
ISBN 0-88106-390-8 (JRB)
[1. Pigeons—Fiction. 2. London (Eng.)—Fiction.]
I. Howard, Kim, ill. II. Title.
P27.S59186Pe 1998
[E]—dc21 97-39074
CIP
AC

Printed in the United States of America
(JRB) 10 9 8 7 6 5 4 3 2 1

The illustrations in this book were done in watercolor and pencil
on Arches 300 lb. paper.
The display type and text type were set in
Domenic, Usherwood and Gibraltar.
Color separations were made by Pre-Press Company, Inc.,
East Bridgewater, Massachusetts
Printed and bound by Worzalla Publishing Company,
Stevens Point, Wisconsin
Art direction by Sallie Baldwin
Production supervision by Brian G. Walker
Designed by Diane M. Earley
This book was printed on recycled paper.

To Caroline, Nick and Cliff, with much love,
and thanks for the inspiration!
—S. S.

For Tante Karen McCall, our forever "amie."
—K. H.

Many pigeons live in
London, but only one is
named Percy. Percy looks
like an ordinary pigeon,
but this is the story of
how he did something
extraordinary.

Like other pigeons, Percy enjoyed visiting
the famous places around the city. He loved
to soar over the Tower of London and see
where kings had kept
their prisoners
long ago.

Percy liked holding one of Big Ben's hands and riding
from three to four. Time flew when Percy was having fun.

Percy liked to glide over Buckingham Palace during the changing of the guard. He had a much better view than the thousands of tourists below.

Percy loved to strut around Trafalgar Square, visit with the other pigeons, and sit atop one of Lord Nelson's lions.

Every day at about five o'clock, Percy flew
past the curving lake called the Serpentine in
Hyde Park to the shore in Kensington Gardens.
The lake had been built by King George the
Second for Queen Caroline hundreds of
years ago.

There, beside a statue of Peter Pan, Percy could always find his friend Matilda. Matilda liked to talk, and Percy was a good listener. He could understand what Matilda was saying, but, alas, he could not answer. Percy could only shake his head yes or no.

One day after Percy had finished the bread
crumbs Matilda always fed him, he headed back
over the Serpentine.

Far below, Percy noticed two boys on an
island in the lake. He could see their boat
floating away, and he heard one boy shouting.

"Cliff, look!" cried the boy. "There goes our boat! I thought I tied it up. Now how are we going to get home?"

"Let's yell for help, Nicholas," said his younger brother. "Maybe someone will hear us."

"HELP! Somebody help us!" shouted the boys.

But it was no use. It was getting dark, and everyone else on the lake had already returned their boats to the boathouse. No one noticed the boys' predicament. No one, that is, except Percy.

Suddenly, Nicholas heard a flapping sound. He turned to see Percy landing on the ground beside him.

"Look, Cliff, a pigeon! Maybe he could carry a message for us!"

"I have some crayons and paper in my backpack!" said Cliff, wiping away his tears.

But Nicholas looked sadly at the pigeon and said, "You can't help us, little bird. You don't know how, do you?"

Percy nodded his head up and down. "Did you see that, Cliff!" Nicholas exclaimed.

Cliff asked, "Can you hear me?" And Percy nodded his head yes.

"Can you take a message to help us?" Nicholas asked. Once again, Percy's head bobbed up and down.

Nicholas quickly wrote a message on Cliff's paper.

Before Nicholas could even fold the paper, Percy
grabbed it in his beak and flew off toward the boathouse.
Tap, tap, tap! Percy rapped his beak on the window
of the boathouse, but the ticket office was closed for
the day. Everyone had gone home.

So Percy flew into town. He spotted a smartly dressed lady stepping out of Harrods department store. He dove down to her, flapping his wings noisily to make her notice the note.

"Oh shoo! Shoo!" screamed the lady. "My new hat! Get away from me! SHOO!"

Percy flew away, discouraged. Then he thought of something. The Palace guards! They would rescue the boys.

As fast as he could, Percy flew to one of the guards he'd seen outside Buckingham Palace. He landed on his busby and waved the note.

No response.

Percy hopped to the guard's shoulder. Nothing. No matter what Percy did, the guard stood at attention and ignored him.

Percy flew on, frantic to find someone to help. Then he remembered . . .

. . . MATILDA! Percy flew straight to Kensington
Gardens to find his friend. He was just in time.
Matilda was getting ready to go home.

"Blimey! Didn't expect to see you back till feedin' time tomorrow," said Matilda. "What's that you've got, eh?"

Percy dropped the note and Matilda read the message.

" 'Op on me shoulder," she said. "We'll get the bobbies, and you'll lead 'em to the boys."

The boys cheered and waved happily
as Percy led the bobbies to the rescue.

The next day Percy was the most
famous pigeon in all the land.

To show her appreciation for Percy's heroic feat, the queen gave him a regal roost in the gardens at Buckingham Palace. The queen also gave Matilda permission to visit Percy for high tea whenever she liked.

And every so often, Percy would be asked to carry a very special message for someone at Buckingham Palace who was even more famous than Percy.

DISCARD

Albany St.

London Zoo

Regents Park

Park Rd.

Marylebone Rd.

Oxford St.

Bayswater Rd.

Hyde Park

Park Lane

Peter
Pan's
statue

The Serpentine

Kensington
Gardens

Buckingham
Palace

Kensington Rd.

Knightsbridge

Harrods

Vauxhall Bridge

Cromwell Rd.

King's Rd.

Chelsea Embankment

The Thames

E·R